Maurice Saxby, expert on Australian literature for young people, said he often wondered why so many adults cherish their battered and wounded teddy bears, and why bears had become metaphors of a certain type of childhood. Some time ago, he wrote in a review, 'It was when Robert Ingpen's first grandchild, Sarah Louise, was born that Ted and Teddy were taken out of their boxes and sat on a chair to engage the heart of a new generation.' What would the bears be thinking? What would they say to each other? Robert Ingpen overheard that conversation and wrote it down, to be published as a story with pictures in 1986. *The Idle Bear* has remained in print in many languages, and now Sarah Louise has a daughter, Rose, who will soon have a new bear story to celebrate her birth.

The Age of Acorns recalls an event in Robert's childhood when Ted, his bear, was left stranded one night in the old oak tree of his family home in Geelong. Bear recounts his fears of meeting the strange people from next door. There are Belladonna Snagglefang, the sacking doll stuffed with wheat husks, and Jenny Greenteeth, the Story Witch, and her terrible cat Modestine. In telling his version of that night, Bear invites us to see more clearly the often formless fears of childhood.

In between is *A Bear Tale*, another adventure that Ted wants us humans to know about. The old bear lives in a corner of a spare bedroom with other family toys, where grandchildren sleep when they visit. Ted tries to find out what wisdom is, and travels across the bedroom to seek advice from a community of ornamental owls that live on a dressing table. They have been lovingly collected from all over the world by Robert's wife Angela. In this version of the old parable, Ted is reminded that home, in friendly, familiar surroundings, is good for wisdom.

The Robert Ingpen Collection

Originally published by Thomas C. Lothian as:
The Idle Bear © Robert Ingpen 1986
A Bear Tale © Robert Ingpen 2000
The Age of Acorns © Robert Ingpen 1988

This combined edition first published 2004

Thomas C. Lothian Pty Ltd
132 Albert Road, South Melbourne, Victoria 3205
www.lothian.com.au

National Library of Australia
Cataloguing-in-Publication data:

Ingpen, Robert 1936- .
The Robert Ingpen Collection.

For children
ISBN 0 7344 0765 3.

1. Children's stories, Australian. I. Title.

A823.3

Printed in China through Colorcraft Ltd, Hong Kong

The Robert Ingpen Collection

THE IDLE BEAR
A BEAR TALE &
THE AGE OF ACORNS

The Idle Bear

"What kind of a bear are you?" asked Ted.

"I'm an Idle Bear."

"But don't you have a name like me?"

"Yes, but my name is Teddy. All bears like us are called Teddy."

Ted thought for a while, then said, "Well, Teddy, I have been Ted forever— at least fifty years, I think."

"Me too," said Teddy, "at least that long."

We could be related, thought Ted and Teddy together.

"We are related!" announced Ted, pretending he had known for ages.

"How can you tell, Ted?" challenged Teddy, "How do you know?"

"Oh, I just know. Everybody has relations, I think especially where I come from," said Ted beginning to wish it wasn't so.

"Where do you come from, Ted?"

"From an idea," said Ted definitely.

"But ideas are not real, they are only made-up," said Teddy. "You have to come from somewhere real to have realitives."

"Not realitives, relatives!" said Ted trying to hide his confusion.

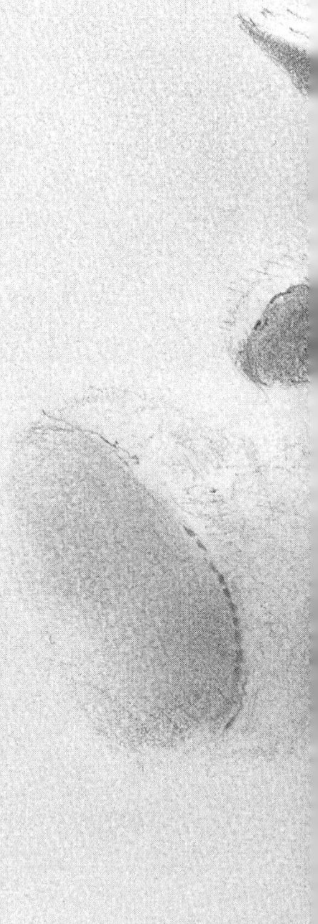

Ted remembered that everybody he had met had come from 'up the street', and said, "I come from up the street."

"What street?" questioned Teddy.

In desperation Ted said, "Up the street next to your street."

"What happens up the street?"

"That depends," said Ted, now really confused, "That depends on everything else that happens."
That should do, thought Ted.

"Like what?" demanded Teddy.

Ted tried to remember. "When I was young,"
he began, "I used to have a lot to do.
I was as important as a bear can be,"
Ted paused, then went on,
"later I was put away, and taken out,
and put away, and taken out, and put . . ."

"Put away where?" interrupted Teddy.

"In a box."

"What sort of a box? A bear box?"

"I don't know," said Ted, "just a box."

"Oh," said Teddy.

"Have you got a growl?" said Ted.

"I used to have one but it wore out," said Teddy.

"Mine still works," said Ted proudly, "at least I think it does."

"Don't you know?"

"That depends," said Ted, "that depends on what I do. If I stand like this it works sometimes."

Ted stood on his head as best he could.

Then he bent backwards.

"It's something to do with my tummy, but I've never seen it," Ted said and stood on his head again.

"It's a very small growl, Ted," said Teddy.

"It's better than a worn out growl," said Ted feeling challenged again.
"It used to be very loud.
I used to be full of growl
when I was young,
up the street."

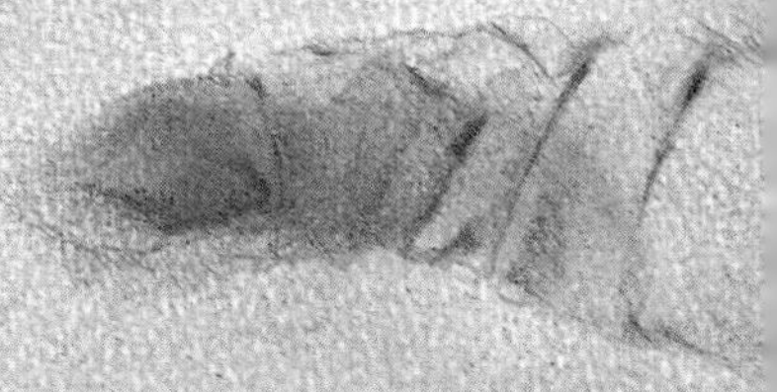

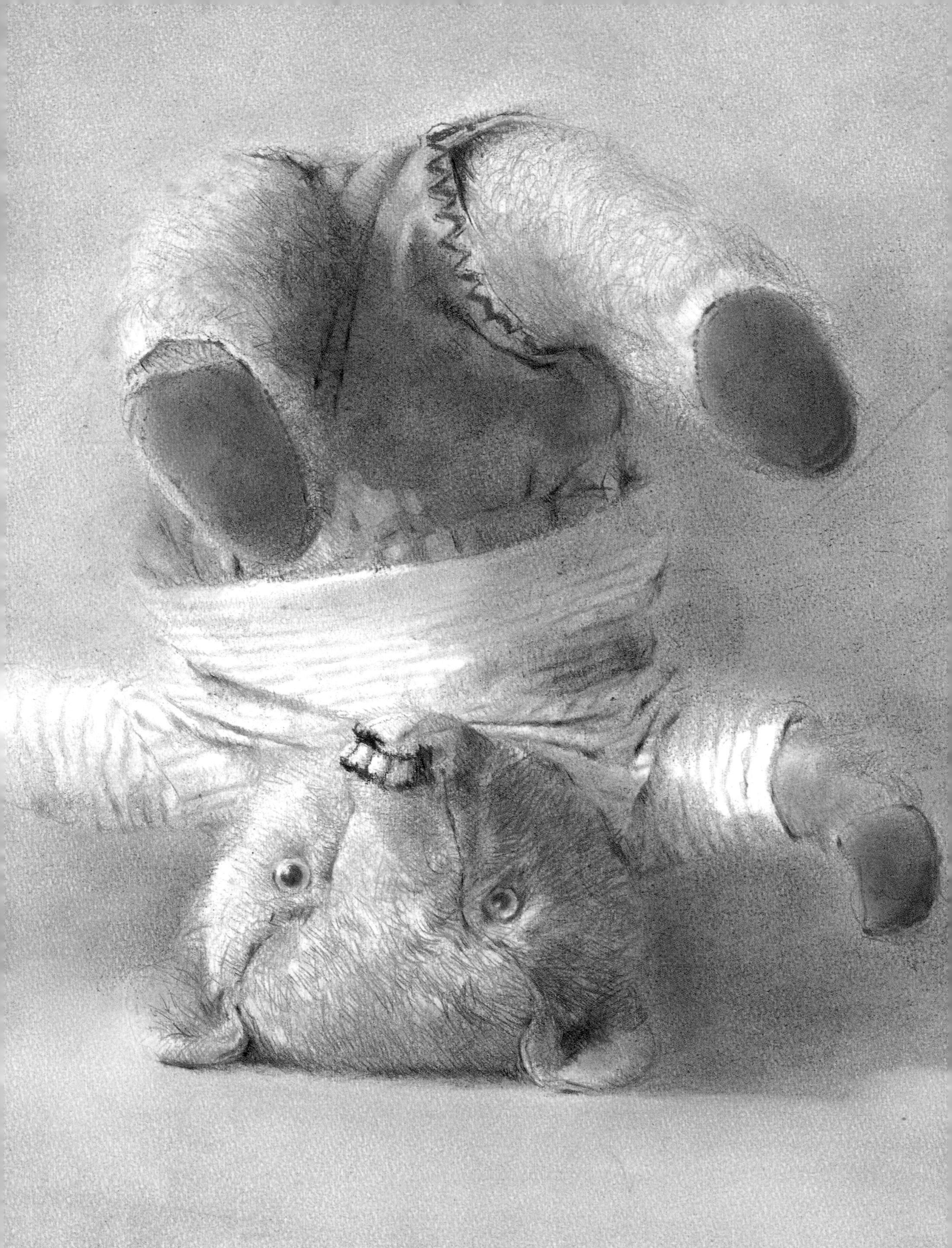

''I'm full of straw,'' announced Teddy.

Ted ignored that. It sounded reasonable and anyhow he was probably full of straw too, if they were related. But then scarecrows and cushions are full of straw and the thought of being related to a cushion annoyed him.

Ted was still thinking about cushions and scarecrows when Teddy startled him by saying, ''Dogs.''

''What about dogs?'' said Ted.

"Dogs come from up the street,"
announced Teddy.

Ted thought, *of course they do,*
and remembered Michael.
He hadn't seen Michael for how long?
"It must be forty years," thought Ted aloud.

"What?" said Teddy.

"It must be forty years since I've seen Michael,
I wonder where he is?"

"Michael who?"

"Michael Wood, the dog next door,
up the street."

"Oh," said Teddy.

"Why do you wear that bandage?" asked Teddy.

Ted looked sadly at his bandaged wrist. "Oh, just because my paw wore out," he said.

"Like my growl wore out, I suppose," suggested Teddy, glad that Ted was not perfect.

"I suppose," said Ted still searching for a clever reply. Then he had an idea.

"It gives me a worldly look," he explained.

"What does?" demanded Teddy.

"My bandage on my worn out paw," said Ted. "With that and me together," he went on, "I am a Worldly Bear." He remembered that somebody once had admired him, and shaken him, and told him he was a worldly bear.

"What's a worldly bear?" asked Teddy.

"One that's worldly," said Ted wisely. He was quite content just being worldly without having to explain what it meant — that's part of being worldly.

"I'm an Idle Bear," said Teddy.

"I know," said Ted, "You told me so."

"Don't you want to know what an Idle is?"

"No," said Ted.

"My owner is an Idle," said Teddy ignoring Ted, "so I'm an Idle too."

Ted wished he knew what an Idle was.

And he is still thinking about it.

A Bear Tale

As Ted the Bear sat with all the other toys in the corner of the bedroom, he thought about getting comfortable.

'I can sit up straight,' he said to nobody in particular. 'I can lie on my back, or on my front, but slumping is best. I do a slump because it sounds comfortable — I like the way it sounds.'

So he said it three times, quite loudly, 'Slump, slump, slump.'

Once someone saw him slumping and commented, 'What a wise old bear you seem to be.'

And, of course, Ted agreed he was, and felt pleased that the others noticed how wisely he slumped. To him it sounded rather good to be old and wise, particularly when you could also be comfortable.

He knew about old, because he had grown up gradually becoming old. His nose was worn, one eye was loose, a paw was bandaged and his growl had gone.

But he really needed to know what wise meant.

So he started asking about wisdom.

'How do you get it?' he questioned various toys. 'Where does it come from? What does it look like?'

None of the toys knew for sure, not even Joey the Dog.

Joey said that he had once heard that owls were wise, and so they would probably know what wisdom was and how you could get some. He advised Ted, 'If you go and talk to the owls, they will surely be able to answer your questions.'

The owls were a collection of ornaments who lived in a semi-circle on a table in the far corner, right across the bedroom. Their owner had collected them on her visits to worldly places. She had arranged them in such a way that they might be expected to answer questions, give advice and sometimes make judgements.

There were owls from everywhere — from Mexico, England, Germany and even Taiwan — owls made of pottery, china, wood and cloth.

With quite a big effort, Ted left his home in the corner and made his way as best he could across the bedroom to the owls' table.

Without any greeting or preamble, he addressed the collection of owls. 'If I am a wise bear, how can I tell?'

There was no answer, so he repeated the question.

Still no answer.

'Perhaps they are dumb, or deaf,' he thought, and was just about to ask for the third time, in a louder voice, when the fluffy young German owl spoke softly.

'We can't tell you.'

'Why not?' said Ted, feeling a little uncomfortable and sorry that he had left home. He felt even worse when there was silence once again.

After a long while, the brown English owl with a ring in his nose began what was to be a long, rambling, speech. 'We can't tell you,' he repeated. 'We can't tell you because we do not know. We owls have been seeking the answers to all the questions about wisdom since Han Owl was born. That was ages ago, and we still don't know.'

Then he went on and on about looking for wisdom, until he finally interested Ted by saying something he could understand.

'We *can* tell you this,' the English owl announced. 'We owls are often told that if we go to a place crowded with toys, like dolls, dogs and bears and things, we will be told the answers. But that, of course, is nonsense.'

'Why is that nonsense?' said Ted, now feeling rather hurt. He tried to comfort himself by slumping, but English Owl made that difficult by saying, 'Because they — the toys — could not possibly know anything. It would be a waste of time asking.'

Ted was just on the point of getting up and leaving the company of owls when he was surprised to hear himself say, 'How do you *know* that we toys would not know?'

He felt good challenging the owl.

'Well,' said a voice from the back of the group. It was Han Owl, the ancient Chinese bowl owl, and he spoke in Mandarin. 'It is well known that all toys slump, and slumping and wisdom never go together. Either you slump, or you are wise — you can't have both. That's why there is no point in asking toys about wisdom, and where it comes from, and all those things. We owls know this.'

With that, Ted returned home to the toys in the other corner of the bedroom. He worried all the way about what Han Owl had said. If he was to be comfortable, he needed to slump. Yet if he was wise he shouldn't slump, because if he did, everybody would think he had no wisdom. Could it be possible to be comfortable and wise as well?

Back in his corner, the toys greeted him as if he had returned from a long, heroic journey, and he told them all that had happened with the owls.

When he had completely finished, all the toys settled down again as if nothing had happened. From then on, though, they noticed that Ted was not slumping as much as before, and he appeared to be further lost in thought than ever.

It even seemed to some that he had decided to arrange himself in such a way that he might be expected to answer questions, give advice and sometimes make judgements.

The Age of Acorns

Bear was deep in thought.

The Others had sat him high in the old oak tree to be what they called 'a lookout'. He had been told to watch out for dragons, and that was just what he had been doing during the game.

Being deep in thought was the thing he most liked to do. Thinking is what a bear like him does best. He was so good at thinking after many years of practice that he could pretend to be doing something else at the same time. The Others — the children who made up the games — never knew what he was thinking about. But they knew he was thinking.

It was the end of summer. Bear was thinking deeply about how good it would be if summer could last all the year. Now was the time he liked most of all. The time when most happened in the garden around the old oak tree. For Bear it was the Age of Acorns.

The acorns that formed among the green oak leaves around his lookout branch had begun to turn brown and to loosen from their cups. Every now and then an early one would fall through the canopy of leaves and go 'plop' on the garden far below.

Summer would become autumn when all the acorns fell to the ground. Next, the leaves would change their green to brown and then fall. The tree would be bare, and it would be winter.

And, thought Bear, if the Others didn't soon remember to fetch him to take him inside he might have to stay in the tree while all that happened around him.

Sometime earlier the Others had been called into the house for tea. Usually he would have been gathered up and taken inside. But that evening he had been left behind, and would have to remain where he was until someone remembered him.

Even as it grew dark Bear could still see the house where the Others had gone. He could hear their chatter and the sounds of tea.

There were always four children who played the games that needed him, two who lived in the house, and two who came from up the street.

Once Bear had heard one of the children say that any good game had to have a bear in it. So he felt needed and important. But now it was becoming cold and dark, and Bear felt forgotten as he looked down through the leaves and gloom into the garden.

He looked in the direction of the back fence and could just see the walnut tree in the corner where 'The Nasties' came under the fence with their tanks and bombs and things, when it suited the Others. Along one side of the garden, beyond the clothes line and lavender hedge, was a cherry plum tree and an artichoke forest. Then, beyond that, were the Woods, the strange world of next door.

Bear felt sure one of the Others would come to fetch him as an excuse to get out of doing homework, or at the last moment between teeth-time and bed-time. Otherwise he would have to stay outside all night, and strange things happen in the garden at night. He knew that.

So, being a thinker, he tried not to think forward, and thought backwards. He thought about the game of Castles and Dragons that had been played in the usual way that afternoon. From his lookout place in the highest turret of the castle he could still imagine most of the battlefield. In his own special way he thought that he could see the retreating enemy through the smoke haze of cannon fire that wafted around the fortress walls.

Bear knew the enemy well. They had attacked many times after school during earlier ages of acorns. The Others knew them as dragons, and Bear supposed this was because they couldn't see what they were from his point of view. He could make them be any enemy he wanted them to be. He supposed that was why he was always given the part of Lookout-in-Games.

That afternoon, as usual, the dragons had been defeated. The weary knights and maidens had gone inside, and the smoke of battle began to smell like burning acorns in the incinerator near the back gate.

Night settled gently around the forgotten bear like reality after a dream. Bear tried not to think of the night, but further ahead to tomorrow. He guessed, as best he could, about what game the Others would choose to play after school tomorrow. If it was to be Pirates and Galleons there would be planks to walk. It might be Cowboys and Indians with arrows and scalpings and lots of noise. It could even be the game of Space Flights to Far Galaxies and he would do his special space walk.

Bear chose the Pirate Game to think about. The Others would raise 'The Jolly Roger' on the highest branch, and the tree would instantly become a pirate ship. There would be wooden swords and black eyepatches, and a treasure of golden acorns wrapped in silver paper to bury. Later, captives would be taken and teased with live beetles in matchboxes. Then he, the crow's nest lookout bear, would be taken down and tied up and made to walk the plank.

The game was always the same, and Bear knew his part in it like the back of his paw. It was the way of pirates' play.

Returning from thought, he noticed that it was quite dark. He could not see all the house, only the lights in some windows. Two lights downstairs, and one in the big bedroom upstairs, the one he should now be sharing with the rest of the toys belonging to the Others.

He thought about the house. From the outside it was two-storied, but inside in its rooms Bear knew of many stories. Just like me, Bear thought wisely. On the outside, just one thoughtful bear, but inside him somewhere is a whole lot of things he can think about, and remember, and forget, and even make up.

Outside the safety of the house strange things can happen in the garden at night. Strangers with unfamiliar games can use the garden for play while you sleep. Another world can come to visit.

Bear shivered a little shake that he copied from the children. The kind you make when you think of something scary. The shiver you do when pretending to be cold not frightened.

Bear shivered because he thought he saw a light in the artichoke forest by the fence that divided his world from where the

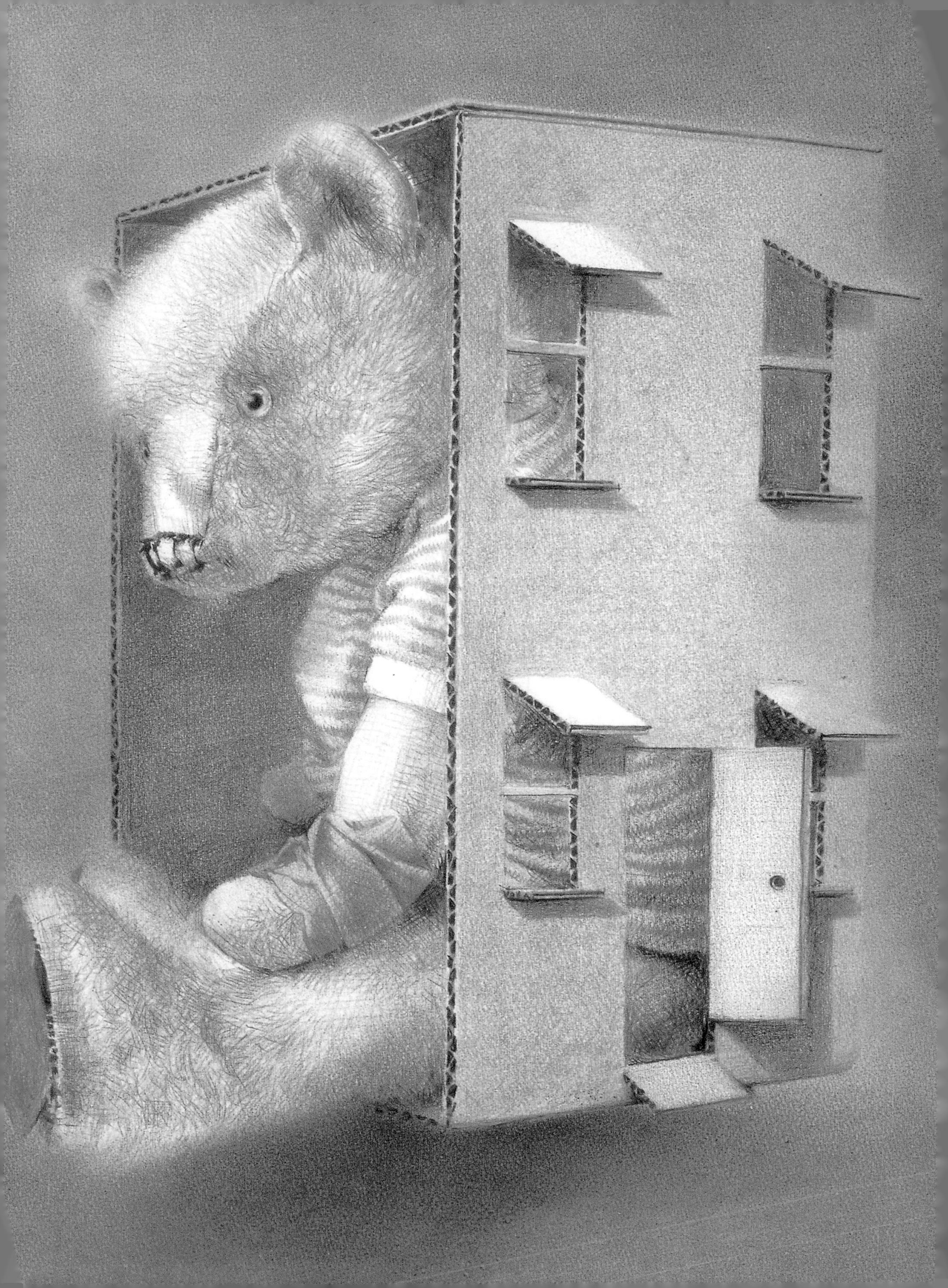

Woods family lived. The strange light danced about as if carried by somebody he couldn't see. He watched it weave its way around the clothes hung out on the line, then through the lavender hedge and out on the open garden. He watched it come to rest below his branch in the old oak tree.

Just then the moon appeared from behind a cloud to give him more light to see. And there they were! Four creatures stood in a group around the light directly below him. He clearly saw an old wrinkled woman dressed in green oak leaves that seemed to be sown on her like a patchwork quilt. She was holding a white lily which produced the scary yellow light. And she was pointing directly at him!

Beside her was Michael the sad dog who belonged to the Woods family. Beside him crouched Modestine the calculating cat. She also belonged to the Woods, when she wasn't away wandering.

The fourth member of the group was Belladonna Snagglefang. Bear had heard the Others talk of her but, until now, he had never seen her. She had been made by one of the Woods family out of old sacks, rope and bright paint. Her long body was stuffed full of wheat husks which spilt on the ground leaving a trail as she moved. She was looking up at him. They were all looking up at him!

Bear knew this was no game he had ever played before. It was something new, and he was frightened. They made no sound at all, and all the games he knew made sounds.

He wasn't really scared of Michael the sad dog or Modestine the cat because, until now, they had never shown much interest in a bear like him. But he felt quite unsure of the ugly doll Belladonna. She moved about as if she was alive, yet her painted face remained a fixed stare.

The sight of the old woman in green was the thing that gave him fear. She was clearly the one in control of whatever game they were about to play.

Then she spoke. 'Bear,' she cackled, 'Bear, down you be coming. We have a game, a new game, to teach you. Down you be coming, Bear.' And her voice tailed off to a fearful laugh.

The next thought that Bear had was so tightly squashed between fear on each side that it was hardly a thought at all. For, as she had spoken he had seen her teeth. They were green! Green as the leaves that made the clothes she wore. Instantly he knew that she must be Jenny Greenteeth the Story Witch. And she was in his garden, his world.

Until now Jenny Greenteeth had only appeared in a story. One called *Giantland* which was sometimes read to the Others by somebody in the Woods family.

A scary story to be told only when the children were safely tucked into bed inside the house.

Bear and the other toys pretended not to be listening to the tales told of that evil witch. That's what toy corners in children's bedrooms are for.
For overhearing stories. He had always been sure she was too evil ever to come out of a story and be real. But now he could see he had been wrong.

She beckoned to him as only witches can. With a long twiggy finger which seemed to have green slime dangling from it, she beckoned him down from his familiar place high in the tree.

He watched the slimy finger in the lily light and the moon, and felt himself moving to obey her command. He had never ever done that before, he thought, as he moved to get up. He'd never actually moved without help before.

Bear trembled unsteadily as he reached down for the branch below, and then the next.

Then there came a familiar sound, a comforting sound that often broke up the games the Others played. The back door of the house was opened and somebody he knew was coming at last to bring him inside.

They had remembered him. He was no longer forgotten. As he waited now to be rescued he looked down again at the terrible group. A cloudlike mist had begun to swirl around to hide them. The kind of mist, he thought, in which anything might happen — where nothing is, but thinking makes it so.

And they just faded away altogether.

Safely inside the house, comfortable now in his corner with the other toys, Bear was still shivering. Not a pretended or copied one, but one of his very own. He was thinking about what had happened, and what might have happened in the garden that night.

And he is still thinking about it.